A
SLAVE'S
STORY

Saga of a Lost Family

C. EVANS

authorHOUSE®

AuthorHouse™
1663 Liberty Drive
Bloomington, IN 47403
www.authorhouse.com
Phone: 1 (800) 839-8640

Published by AuthorHouse 11/01/2016

ISBN: 978-1-5246-4843-5 (sc)
ISBN: 978-1-5246-4842-8 (e)

Library of Congress Control Number: 1-3309306611

Print information available on the last page.

I dedicate this novel to my two sons, Joshua and Darius, who are my number one fans, my five grandchildren—Aliayah, Damari, Damarion, Darius Jr and Joshua Jr—who I adore, to my cousin and best friend, Margo, who always saw my vision, to my youngest sister, Charlene Clay, my prayer partner, and to La'Duena Gunn, and Devin Hill for helping me critique this story. Much love and may God bless you all.

CONTENTS

PREFACE

One early morning in October of 2014, I awoke because of a dream. The dream was about a young girl walking along a path behind a big house. She was passing a small cabin when she heard sounds from inside. The young girl appeared to be white, and the times seemed to be during the Negro slavery days. As I thought of the dream, a voice within me said, "Write down everything you remember." So, I found a notebook and pen, and I began to write this story. I wrote for several months. The title and the entire story came into my mind, and the words flowed through my pen. It was a story that wanted to be told.

This is a story of a young girl born into slavery bondage, who was the daughter of a Negro slave woman and the plantation master. She tells her life's journey from slavery to freedom, and how she got away with things that other Negro slaves could not, and it recounts her losses all along the way.

CHAPTER 1

I was born into slavery, the daughter of Mae, my mother, who was a lost soul. All my years of growing up, she would sit in her cabin, and rock back and forth. My grandmother took care of me, and was the overseer of all the young single women on the plantation. Our cabin was the first one, before a long line of small cabins in the women's quarters. Massa made sure he kept the single women and men apart from each other, as to keep down the population of the slaves.

Massa John Roberts was his name, and he had a wife that died giving birth to his second son, who was my age. Massa was a tall and stern man, who seemed to have a soft side toward me. As a young girl, I never did much work like the other slave children my age did. They worked in the fields and in the Big House all day. Some tended to animals, while others cleaned, dusted, and helped with the cooking in the Big House. As a little girl, I just ran around and played, and most of the other girls disliked me for that. So, I had only one or two friends who would play with me when their work was done.

My grandmother named me *Belle* because she said, the supper bell was ringing in the Big House the moment I was being born. Grandmother was a tall, very dark woman with wide hips, and long thick black hair that she kept in a braid going down her back. She had a loud voice that could be heard miles away, and she was also allowed to yell at the slave women, and take them to the whipping post if any got out of sorts. Grandmother also took care of me, but she never whipped me.

My mother lived in a cabin off by itself at the end of a long path that led right up to the Big House. She never did any work because she was sick in the head. So, grandmother took care of her also. She would take her food to eat, keep her clean, and comb her hair. Mother was also tall with tan colored skin, along with dark wavy hair, and a curvy body with full breasts. She had a pretty face with long eyelashes which made grandmother often say, "You get them eyes from your mother, gal!"

I wondered why mother wasn't right in the head, but grandmother said, she got like that because she had two baby boys before me that died. I would often go and visit mother, and during them times she would brush my hair and sing to me. I liked those moment because I felt she knew who I was, but she always had a faraway look in her eyes. Then, when dusk came, she would push me out of her cabin. Grandmother said I was never to be there at night, and I could never sleep there with her. For a long time, I didn't understand that.

My skin's a lot lighter than my mother's and my grandmother, who was called Rose. My legs are long, so I guess I'd be tall like them. My hair is very long and curly, and almost as light as my skin. I like to wear it down and loose, but grandmother would always give me a braid, like her. My eyes were light brown, so light that the other slave women would say, "Them eyes of hers are gone bring her much grief."

I didn't understand that either, and they never said it around grandmother Rose.

My life was easy, until I reached the age of ten. Then I started to work, but not as hard as the other slave children my age did. I tended to the small animals, and often was called into the Big House to cook and clean. Whenever I went to the Big House to work, Massa Roberts would reward me with things, like ribbons for my hair and an apron to wear. One time, he even gave me a pretty, plain dress. I liked it when he gave me things, but the other slaves didn't like it at all and would say mean things to me often. I didn't understand why he did this, and it went on for several years. Grandmother said it was okay to take them things, but to keep my mouth shut about them.

Massa Roberts had two sons. The oldest had his father's name and was five years older than his brother, whose name was James. Massa James was friendly to everyone, but his brother was stern and mean to the slaves. I would often talk and play with Massa James, but when his brother was around I was not allowed to.

When I reached the age of thirteen, grandmother took ill and was not able to care for my mother anymore. Then I had to care for her. I took mother her food, brushed her hair, and kept her clean. She never talked, only hummed, and sang two songs over, and over. I got used to it.

A young slave girl tended daily to my grandmother, since I worked in the big house after seeing and tending to my mother. So often it would be dusk when I left there ... which brings me to the night that changed my life forever.

It was dusk out, and I had walked down the path from the Big House that led to my mother's cabin. I heard heavy breathing, and it sounded like my mother was crying very low, as if she didn't want to be heard. Then I walked up to the window and saw a candle burning inside, which made it easy for me to see. I should've went on, but I wanted to know what was wrong with her.

As I looked inside, I saw Massa Roberts and my mother, both naked. He was on her, holding her face and neck, like a mad dog in heat! I burst in and began to beat his back. I yelled, "Get off her!" He rolled off, then turned and slapped me to the floor.

For the first time, I heard my mother speak as she yelled, "GET OUT BELLE!"

Massa Roberts stood in front of me naked, and I saw all his man parts. I was so scared. I jumped up to run out, but I looked at his face; he had a look of sorrow, as if it hurt him what he did to me. I ran to grandmother's cabin crying. When I got there my grandmother said, *"Hush gal.* What them tears for?"

I began to tell her what had happened.

"Hush, don't say no more," she said.

I couldn't understand why she was not upset, cause Massa Roberts had hurt my mother in a bad way. Grandmother was not feeling good cause she was getting old in age, and her body was not doing well. She was lying down on her cot when I got there.

She sat up and said, "Massa Roberts owns us, and we are his property, and he does what he wants with us, but he's a good Massa. Hush them tears, and never go to your mother's cabin at night again, and NEVER speak of this." I didn't understand this, and I thought to myself, I would never forgive Massa Roberts or take any of his gifts again.

CHAPTER 2

As time went by I continued to take care of my mother during the mornings, and I never spoke about that night. Mother became more lost in the head. She wouldn't hum or sing anymore, and she never spoke my name again. She only sat by the window, and rocked back and forth. As the year went by, she wouldn't eat much food, and she got weaker, and weaker.

After I made fourteen, Mother died at the age of thirty-one. She was buried in the slave's graveyard not far from our cabin, and grandmother put some pretty flowers on her grave.

I continued to work most of the days in the Big House, and Massa Roberts made me learn to sew and cook very well. I would often make cookies for Massa James, and we would sit on the back steps of the big house and talk to each other for long spells. Sometimes Young Massa Roberts would catch us, and yell at me, saying I would be whipped at the whipping post.

Massa James would always yell back at his older brother, "You will never touch her!" So, we would have to be careful most of the time.

My grandmother was still alive when I reached fifteen in age, but she was barely able to move about, and she was having trouble seeing. Even though she was only fifty-one years in age, her body had been through much hard work. Her fingers had become bent and her legs weak. She couldn't do much work anymore, and Massa Roberts never pushed her to. The young slave girl continued to care for grandmother, along with me helping. A lot of the children would come around her, as she became the story teller of the days of old.

One morning, on my way to the Big House, I passed the cabin my mother used to live in. I saw that it was being repaired. I wondered why, because it sat empty for a while now, but I never spoke about it. When I got to the Big House, I saw young Massa Roberts giving me them looks like he would often do.

I was now tall for my age, and had come into my womanhood, with full breasts, hips and long legs. Massa James and me would always race, but I would out run him all the time. He would often say, "It's them long legs of yours. They're like a horse."

We had become close in friendship, as we grew up together.

One morning, while working at the Big House, not long after my sixteenth birthday, Massa Roberts gave a big party for Massa James's birthday, who made sixteen, also. He made me make new aprons and dresses for all the women slaves who worked for the party that evening. I did such a good job on the clothes, that Massa Roberts gave me a pretty dress with flowers all over it as a gift and I loved it!

Later that evening, as I was going to my cabin, I saw Young Massa Roberts standing in the back along the path. He had that look in his eyes and had been drinking that devil drink. I tried to pass him, but he made me stop. He told me stand still. Young Massa Roberts was a man now, fully grown, twenty-one years in age. He was tall like his daddy, with light brown eyes like mine, and yellow colored hair. He stood over me, with that smell of that devil drink on his breath, and then he grabbed my shoulders to pull me to him.

"Please Young Massa Roberts, I must go tend to my grandmother who is ill," I begged.

He said nothing, and just started touching me the wrong way. I started to cry.

Then I heard Massa James coming around the back of the Big House calling my name, "Belle, where are you?" He came to a stop when he saw his brother holding me. Massa James yelled out, "Take your hands off, of her!"

Young Massa Roberts let me go and walked away, with that look still in his eyes.

"Are you alright? Don't worry Belle. I will never let him hurt you," Massa James said. I ran to my grandmother's cabin and asked her to pray for me, without telling nothing about what happened.

CHAPTER 3

Time went on, and another year was passing. I went to the Big House everyday by way of the path, pass my mother's old cabin. It had been fully repaired, but no one lived there yet. I often wondered who it was fixed for.

As I worked in the Big House, Massa Roberts gave me more charge over the other girls because I had learned to do everything. I also learned to stay out of the way of Young Massa Roberts as much as I could, for he would give me looks that made me so afraid. During these times, Massa James was getting his schooling at the Big House. He was always around, but his eighteenth birthday was coming soon, and he was to leave for more schooling elsewhere. I started to worry more, and more about that day coming because he would no longer be there to stop his brother. I was also eighteen, and considered a grown woman.

Grandmother was up in age, fifty-four years, and she was not doing well at all. Most times she would just sleep the day away, and she was always in pain. I had a feeling that my grandmother would not be around for much longer.

One warm night, everyone was sleeping in the slave quarters. One of the girls from the Big House came running and yelling for me to come with her. She woke up everybody! Grandmother says, "Go see child what the fuss is about!" It was Massa Roberts. He had fallen sick. He was fifty-eight years in age, and several years older than my grandmother. I ran to the Big House, and they had called for the doctor who was already there. Young Massa Roberts and his brother, Massa James were at their daddy's bedside. They said Massa Roberts had a stroke, and it left his body not working on one side, but he was still alive.

The time had come, for Massa James to leave for his schooling. Massa James was tall, but not as tall as his brother. He, too, had them light brown eyes like mine, but his hair was dark brown like his mother. He had grown into a man with a kind face, kind ways, and a gentle soul. I was so sad to see him go, for we had become very close friends, and I had come to love him, even though I dare not say so. We said our goodbyes, and Massa James told me not to worry, for he would be back soon. But in my mind, I knew … here comes the troubles.

They made Massa Roberts a special chair with wheels, so he'd be pushed around, and it was my job to do the pushing. I didn't mind because it kept me away from Young Massa Roberts most of the time. Massa Roberts couldn't talk much anymore, so he made me learn to read and write so that I could talk for him. Then I learned how to write down most things that happened in my life.

Massa Roberts health didn't get much better, so young Massa Roberts started taking care of most things on the plantation, and he was very stern about it.

It was near my twentieth birthday when grandmother's health gave way to her death, at fifty-six years in age. I buried her next to my mother in the old slaves' graveyard. I made a bushel of flowers in a basket and put them on her grave. I cried, and mourned over her for some time. Massa Roberts gave me several days for this, but then he made me come back to the Big House to work, because of being in charge, of most things.

One warm summer day, everyone was surprised by Massa James coming home to visit. But he didn't come alone. I was so happy to see him again. He came with a young lady, and her name was Miss Mary. She was our age, and he said he met her while he was away at school. She was pretty and polite.

Massa James had come home to see how his daddy health was, and to visit his brother. He saw me, and said hi. He spoke of how much of a woman I had become. He thanked me for taking good care of his daddy. While he was visiting, I kept out of the way, for I knew my place in this house. Massa James didn't stay long, and we said our goodbyes. I wasn't so sad this time.

Massa Roberts's health didn't get much better, and he had taken to his bed most times. Me and the other servant girls in the house had to take turns caring for Massa Roberts, day and night.

Young Massa Roberts kept busy most times. He did a lot of traveling, back and forth from the Big House to the town. He was now handling all the plantation business for his daddy. There had been times he'd come home and all the servants would get in a fuss because he wanted things just right. One day he yelled for me to bring his supper into the eating parlor, and he had been drinking that stuff again. I walked in and served his supper, without showing any fear. He made me wait. He said he just wanted to look at me. Young Massa Roberts said, "You done grew into a mighty fine woman!"

I just lowered my head and spoke nothing. Then he waved his hand for me to leave. I went to Massa Roberts's room to check on him to keep from walking home in the dark that night. When Young Massa Roberts went to his room to sleep, I left and went to my cabin. All twenty-two years of my life I had never seen Young Massa Roberts come home with a young lady, or even talk of one. Maybe, on account, of them devil drinks that changed his ways about him.

I had become very tall, with a curvy body, and full breasts like my mother. My skin is as light as Massa Roberts's, and my hair is down my back, and it's almost as light as my skin. I still braided it like Grandmother's, to keep it out of the way. I often wondered, why I am the color I am, and why my hair, and eyes were like this too. I didn't look like any of the other negro slaves.

CHAPTER 4

Massa Roberts's health had gotten really, bad. Then one day, while working in the Big House, he sent for me to come to his room on account, of him having something to say to me. Young Massa Roberts was on one of his traveling trips, so I went to his daddy's bedside. I lowered my head to his mouth so that I could hear what he had to say. What he said made me to feel faint. Massa Roberts said to me he was sorry for hurting my mother all them years, and … he be my Daddy.

Now I understood who I was. He said he was dying and wanted me to know this. Then he said to never tell his sons what he told me, and to never let them touch me, on account, of them being my brothers. I thought to myself, how could he treat me this way, even on his death bed, but he made me promise.

We sent for young Massa Roberts, and his daddy held on till he came to his bedside. Then, Massa Roberts died at sixty-two years in age.

Young Massa Roberts buried his daddy in the family graveyard on the plantation, next to his wife. All the slaves were there. It was a very nice service, but Massa James didn't come to his daddy's burial. Young Massa Roberts became very angry with him about it, too.

After Massa Roberts's death, Young Massa Roberts went traveling for a few days, and I had some peace within. During this time Massa James came back. He talked to me, said he was sorry for missing his daddy's burial service.

He asked me, "How was it?"

I said, very nice.

Young Massa Roberts returned while his brother was there, and there was much anger in the Big House between them. Massa James tried to tell his brother why he wasn't at his daddy's burial service, that he was on travel with Miss Mary, who he was engaged to marry.

So, Massa James stayed a spell and visited his daddy's grave several times. While he was there, Young Massa Roberts took to drinking again. The anger against his brother grew in Young Massa Roberts's heart. He walked around acting as his daddy gave everything to him. If he caught me and Massa James talking, he would yell at me, and make me do some work to keep us apart. I wanted to tell Massa James what his daddy said to me, but I kept my promise.

It came time for Massa James to leave again, and his brother didn't even come out to say goodbye. So, we said our goodbyes. I was so sad that I cried in front of him. He said, "It's going to be alright, Belle."

But I knew in my heart that it wouldn't, and I became fearful for myself.

Two days after Massa James had left, I was leaving the Big House to go to my cabin. It was dusk outside. When I got there my cabin had been stripped bare. I looked around for all my things, but they were gone. I was so scared. I knew I had to travel back to the Big House to find out what happened. I walked the path where my mother's cabin was, and inside there was several candles burning. All my things were there. I sat up all night until I couldn't stay awake anymore.

When morning came, I went to the Big House, afraid of what I was going to hear.

Young Massa Roberts was having his morning meal, and he said to me, "I had your things moved to your mother's cabin so that you could be closer to the Big House."

I nodded my head and said, "Yes, Young Massa Roberts," then went about my daily work.

Later that day, Young Massa Roberts said to me that he was going on one of his traveling trips again for a few days. I felt at peace. My mother's cabin was right nice, and I began to think this wasn't so bad at all.

Young Massa Roberts drinking, had gotten worst, and he never wanted to talk about his brother, especially since he had not heard from him for some time. His twenty-eighth birthday had come and gone. He has never had a young lady over or ever talked of one, maybe on his travels, but never at the Big House. His anger was growing deep, and he was mean to all of us. There was yelling, and bad words said often, and that was only when he wasn't passed out from drinking.

When I became twenty-three in age, the slave men started saying things to me, cause of Young Massa Roberts staying passed out so much. He had not kept his daddy's ways, hadn't kept the men and women slaves apart anymore. Now there was children all over the place.

One night, while I was in my cabin reading a book that I took from the Big House, I heard a noise outside my cabin. I went to see what it was, but, before I could, he pushed his way in—it was Young Massa Roberts.

. I could tell that he had been drinking badly, again. I was scared, but I stood my ground. I asked him if he needed me to work. He said, "NO!" Then, he grabbed me and tore my dress. I started yelling for him to stop—thinking about what his daddy said to me, him being my brother. He never stopped ... not until he had his way.

When it was over, I cried and softly said to him, "I'm your sister."

He then beat me.

"Never say that to me again. You're my *property*, and I can do to you what I will," he said.

And at that moment, I felt my mother's pain.

CHAPTER 5

Young Massa Roberts had stopped drinking, but continued having his way with me, often. He got the plantation back in order again, selling off many slaves and their children for profit. He became a stern Massa, with very mean ways. I became a soulless woman, in my mother's cabin.

Young Massa Roberts replaced me with a young slave girl, with wide hips and big breasts, to work in the Big House. During these times, we heard nothing from Massa James. He was married, and never talked to his brother.

One morning I awoke with a sickness, and I knew I was with child. I was twenty-four in age and going to have a baby.

As the time passed and I grew far along with the baby, I didn't do much work anymore, only for myself in my cabin. Young Massa Roberts let me be as I will on the plantation grounds. Though, he still came to my cabin, and had his way with me from time to time. Sometimes he talked about things, and I would just listen, not saying a word, which made him angry with me most of the time. He never talked about the child.

I was full with child and could feel it moving. I started to feel okay about it, that it was a part of me. I was going to take good care of my baby.

One morning, Young Massa Roberts came to my cabin. He always came at night, so this was not like him. He said he did not want the baby, and when it's born he was going to sell it. I begged him to please let me keep my baby, to raise it up. He said no, then left to go on one of his traveling trips. I cried the rest of the day until I was sick.

I was seven months along, and I had not felt the baby move inside me anymore. I wondered why. I had been having back pains for the last few days. One night, I saw blood run down between my legs. I got worried and sent for one of the slave women, who helps with the babies being born. She came to my cabin. She was an older woman.

She said, "Your baby gone be born, though it's not time yet."

I spent the rest of the night giving birth to a dead baby boy.

I buried him in the slave's graveyard, next to my mother and grandmother. I didn't give him a name. Young Massa Roberts found out about the baby dying, and never said a word. He let me heal in my body for a few months, and then he sent me back in charge of all things, in the Big House. My feelings for Young Massa Roberts was turning into anger, anger and hate, but I dare not let him know this. And so, I would pray about it all the time.

Word came to the Big House from Massa James. His wife, Mrs. Mary, was about to give birth to their first child, but she was not doing well and had taken to bed. It also said, that he was working, for his father-in-law's business, and he was doing very well. This seemed to cheer up Young Massa Roberts a bit.

One day, Young Massa Roberts come back from one of his traveling trips with a young lady. She was about his age. Her name was Miss Sarah. She didn't smile much, and she seemed to have very stern ways, like him. I was happy to see him with her, and I wished he would marry her. She stayed several days, and he was proud to show her all around the place. Then he took her back where she had come from, and we never saw her again. I guess he was mean to her, too.

He began coming back to my cabin, having his way with me again. This kept me sad, but I wouldn't turn to my mother's ways. I just kept praying, cause sometimes I think I wanted to die. I wondered, was this his way of loving me? By the time I made twenty-five in age, I was with child again. This time Young Massa Roberts was letting me keep the baby. I said to him that I would keep working in the Big House while I'm with child. He said only until I'm big and showing.

We hear word from Massa James again. He said his wife, Mrs. Mary, died giving birth to their baby girl, who also died. I was saddened for him. He said he had been working hard with his wife's family business, to help him get over his grief. He said, also, that one day he would come and visit.

I hoped Massa James didn't come to visit—since I was with child by his brother.

My feelings about Young Massa Roberts had calmed, seeing that he never took a wife, and said he only wants to come to me. But me being his sister, I never liked him touching me. It just wasn't right. I kept thinking about the promise I made to his father, but I never spoke of it.

I was big with child again, and I no longer could work in the Big House. One night, I heard the young slave girl, that Young Massa Roberts put in the Big House to take my place, crying on the path by my cabin.

I asked her, "What them tears for?"

She said, "Young Massa Roberts had his way with me, and hurt me really bad." She said he'd also been drinking.

I said to her, "You gone be alright," but she was awful scared to go back.

Then she ran away from me, off to the slave quarters. I started wondering why was Young Massa Roberts drinking again. His ways were so mean when he drank that stuff. The next morning, they found the young slave girl dead in the woods. She was only seventeen years in age They say she took her own life. I prayed for her soul, but I never said nothing to Young Massa Roberts about it.

CHAPTER 6

I was in my last month with child, and I felt it moving all the time, a good sign I thought. I had even made clothes for the baby. Young Massa Roberts had not been coming to my cabin, since I was so big.

The time had come for the birth of the baby, and I was in so much pain. The slave woman who helps with the birthing, stayed with me during the night. I kept screaming ... seemed like it was taking so long for it to come, and I got scared something was wrong, but the baby was born ... It was so small, another boy. My baby didn't have all his fingers on one hand, and his head seemed to be misshaped, but he was moving, so I knew he was alive. I named him John Roberts. Young Massa Roberts was gone again, on one of his traveling trips, so he had not seen the baby, nor was he concerned about it.

For several days, he would not suckle at my breast, and wasn't doing very well. I guessed something wasn't right inside of him. There was no one to help my baby. He fell very ill and died. Again, I buried a child, by my mother's and grandmother's grave. Though this time, he had a name.

After my baby's death, I became very ill. Young Massa Roberts sent for a doctor to come see me. The doctor said I had a scarred and an infected womb, and that I would never be with child again. I quietly thanked the Lord, since it was wrong to have babies with my brother.

Things started getting bad on the plantation. It turned out that Young Massa Roberts had been making bad choices with the property, on them traveling trips he kept taking. Young Massa Roberts kept selling off the slaves and animals to make ends meet. He started drinking again, and started being mean to everybody. And every now and then, I would get a beating, sometimes in the Big House, sometimes in my cabin. Life here was getting very bad.

Young Massa Roberts let go of all the paid white servants on the plantation and put slaves in their places. Now I had charge over things that the white servants usually did, and if it wasn't done right, Young Massa Roberts would beat me something awful.

I was now twenty-seven years in age, and looked like a white woman. Sometimes I thought that I could easily pass for one, if I wasn't on the plantation. I had become very good at reading, writing, baking, and making my own clothes. I understood why old Massa Roberts made me learn these things, so that I could make a living on my own.

We heard word from Massa James again, and it said that he was coming home, this time to maybe stay awhile. Everybody was filled with joy, but Young Massa Roberts didn't seem so happy. I guessed that he didn't want his brother to learn of his bad choices with the plantation.

One night, as I was in my cabin thinking about the preparations for Massa James's arrival, when Young Massa Roberts came in. He had been drinking again, and he stumbled badly, and I got real scared. He started saying things as—if I tried to leave him, he would kill me—that if I got too friendly with Massa James when he arrived, he would kill the both of us. I believed him. He then had his way with me through the night, and hurt me bad. The next day he told me to stay in my cabin, seeing that I could hardly walk. I was sore everywhere. I stayed in my cabin all day crying, and praying ... wanting to die.

The next day Massa James came home. I was fearful, and didn't know how I was going to stay out of Massa James's way, seeing how we had always been good friends. Young Massa Roberts gave me stern looks all day, that made me, more and more nervous.

Massa James had become such a grown man, tall like his brother, but with very calm ways. When he saw me, he hugged me and said, "You are so grown now." He came home with a lot of stuff, like he was going to stay a good while. All the servants fussed about him. Even Young Massa Roberts was happy. I felt some peace knowing that Massa James would be staying.

Later in the day, the two brothers had a big meal together in the parlor, filled with talk and remembering. I was happy, for them both, and happy cause I knew that night I could rest in my cabin peacefully.

The next morning, things were different. Massa James had found out about the property, about his brother's bad choices. There was much anger between them. I felt fear come over me, knowing how mean Young Massa Roberts could be. He told his brother that he was taking care of the property and didn't need his help. Words between the brothers got bad. They just would not get along. Massa James had come into money and wanted to help his brother with the plantation, but young Massa Roberts would not accept his help. I just tried to stay out of both their ways, staying busy with work most of the time.

While Massa James was there, Young Massa Roberts didn't drink as much, and didn't come to my cabin anymore. I had thought that the Lord heard my prayers. Life was not so bad for me now, but in the big house there was always yelling and fighting.

One day Young Massa Roberts took me aside, said that he was going on a traveling trip for two weeks, and I had better keep in mind what he said to me about his brother. I said okay, and said that I would do as he said, while Massa James was there. So, I kept myself working, and out of the way of Massa James.

CHAPTER 7

One day, while working at the Big House, Massa James called me to the eating parlor, said to sit down and talk with him. We had not had the chance to talk until then. He asked how I was doing, asked why I had not got a husband yet? I told him that I worked all the time, and nobody ever made friends with me that way.

Massa James said, "You have become a fine woman, and I can't understand how no one ever noticed."

I just smile and nodded. We talked about his wife and child, and his grief for them. He said that he was going to stay for some time, help get the place right again, even if his brother didn't want his help.

The next day, I left the Big House early and went to my cabin, as to not be in the way of Massa James. It was dusk outside when I heard walking up to my cabin. I thought it might be Young Massa Roberts, home early, but it was Massa James. Fear gripped my heart. He asked if could he come in. I said okay.

"Is it something you need me to do?" I asked.

He just wanted to talk again. He asked me, "When did you move into this cabin?"

I said after his father's death. Then I said to him, "If you needed me to do something, you can just send one of the girls to fetch me. You don't have come yourself."

Massa James just looked at me, with those kind eyes of his, and smiled, then asked, "How is my brother treating you?"

I said okay, but I don't think he believed me. Then Massa James said something that nearly fainted me.

He said, "You know, sometimes I think you could pass for my sister. Your looks are so much like mine, and my brother's." "Good night. If I need something, I'll send one of the girls next time." I felt much better when he said those words.

Young Massa Roberts had come back from his traveling trip and seemed to be a bit calmer. I often wondered what he did on them trips. Later in the day, he called Massa James to the parlor to talk. They seemed calmer with their words this time. Whatever business they talked of, it sounded like they were getting along.

My twenty-eighth birthday came, but I thought nothing of it, just thanked the Lord that I was still alive. Though, on this birthday, Massa James had the slave girl who does the cooking fashion me a cake. No one had ever done this for me. I didn't know if I should be happy or scared. Though, I did know that Young Massa Roberts would dislike this sort of thing. When time came to serve the brothers their evening meal, Massa James said to come and sit with them, to have some cake.

Young Massa Roberts was unhappy about this. "Belle has work to do! Besides, slaves don't sit in the parlor and eat with us!" he said.

Massa James said, "Belle is special. I don't see her as a slave."

I said that I would take some cake with me, as to keep the anger down between them. But even as I was leaving out, I could hear them having words about me still.

Later that night, Young Massa Roberts came to my cabin. I was nervous cause he had not been there in some time. He had been drinking as he tends to do, but not too badly this time, I just wanted him to just go away.

He said to me, "Thank you for obeying me, and not being so friendly with my brother." Then he had his way with me, though, he didn't hurt me like he did most times, and he didn't talk much either. After that, he just left.

I thought about the way he acted this time, being so easy with me— maybe because it was my birthday. I still thought it was wrong, him always touching me, and knowing I'm his sister. I thought it wrong in the Lord's eyes. I also thought of his daddy, and the promise I made to him, that was never kept.

Now that Massa James was there, I thought to tell him about it, but I was too scared of Young Massa Roberts killing us both. I often think that's why the Lord didn't let me keep my babies, because they belonged to my brother. . .

My birthday had come and gone. It was now Massa James's twenty-eighth birthday, and he and Young Massa Roberts had gone on a traveling trip for the next two days. So, the Big House was peaceful … I was happy about that.

When they returned, Young Massa Roberts, had fell ill with a stomach sickness and took to his bed. Massa James charged a slave girl with his care, but Young Massa Roberts sent for me instead. For three nights and days, until he had gotten better, I stayed to his bedside.   Massa   James disliked his brother's treatment of me, even though I told him I didn't much mind it. Once Young Massa Roberts was fully better, Massa James gave words to his anger.

Young Massa Roberts said in return, "Belle is my business and none of yours." This only gave rise to more of the shouting, and fussing in the Big House.

Days later, word arrived to the Big House for Massa James. His wife's father had died. Massa James had to take leave, to attend his father in law's burial. He said he would be gone for nearly a month.

Then, to Young Massa Roberts, he said, "I want to take Belle with me, to help out." A sudden fear squeezed at my heart, and I nearly lost the balance from my feet.

"Belle will never leave this land!" said Young Massa Roberts.

Massa James just stared at me, then said "I will be back, Belle." We said our goodbyes. The whole time, Young Massa Roberts never once looked at me; this made me cold and afraid. I knew he was upset, and that I would it feel it later. My mind went to prayer all the rest of that day.

Two nights later, Young Massa Roberts visited my cabin, smelling of strong drink. I begged him not to touch me, saying this was a sin in the Lord's eyes. No less, he beat me, and had his way with me harshly. He became very angry.

"Never repeat that to me again! We harbor no kinship!" he said. I cried until he left and thought of taking my own life, and thought of the ease, of an end to this heartache. I had become tired of going on this way ... maybe, I could run, and escape ... maybe I could tell Massa James the truth, about what his daddy said, for many times the promise had already been broken.

CHAPTER 8

Massa James ended up not returning for two months nearly. And when he returned, he had a guest, his wife's mother.

"She's ill, and she'll be staying with us until she's better, and until her grief for her husband has settled," he said. Her name was Mrs. Lilly, and she was sixty-nine years in age. She was a woman very small, in size yet able to move about fairly, well. In fact, she didn't look at all ill to me. Young Massa Roberts agreed to her stay and told me to help her as needed. Mrs. Lilly had a kind face and kinder, blue eyes. She's was calm and soft-spoken, and friendly to me. So, I didn't much mind tending to her.

Massa James showed a tender side for Mrs. Lilly. He told us that she was going to be there for a short while only, that she had a younger sister who would be sending for her. Mrs. Lilly had one child only, Massa James's wife, Mrs. Mary, who had passed. Now, that her husband had died, she had no one.

Young Massa Roberts and Massa James were taking well to one another. I guessed Mrs. Lilly's stay had made them mindful of their manners.

Mrs. Lilly moved about well. She enjoyed sitting in the eating parlor, by the windows, during the day, though Massa James often wished that she would take to her bed.

"I'm not dead! and the living like to walk," she would say.

I tended to her hair, cleaned her, and helped her move about—though she didn't much need it. She had a kind soul, but, at times, she would look at me strangely. A sharp woman: I think my looks made her wonder about things.

It was Young Massa Roberts's thirty-third birthday. Massa James had a large meal prepared and even a cake made. He had the slave girls bring out spirits to drink, and had lighted the Big House bright with candles. It was something to see. Mrs. Lilly, who had become like a mother to them, joined them in the eating parlor. Many nights, I secretly thanked God for her stay. That was a joyous night in the Big House.

One day, Mrs. Lilly was eating breakfast, when she said to me, "Come, sit and talk with me." Young Massa Roberts didn't pay mind to me sitting and talking with Mrs. Lilly, just as long, as my day's work was finished. She stared at me strangely, in that way she sometimes did, and asked, "Are you a paid white servant?" I said that I was just a slave, born on the plantation, and was not white. She said nothing more, just nodded and left it at that.

That evening, word spread that two slaves, a young man and woman, had run off together. Young Massa Roberts, Massa James, and a handful of slave men, with two bloodhounds set off after them. Though the plantation spread wide and far, by morning light they had found them.

Young Massa Roberts, had the both, of them tied to the posts and whipped them to near death, that is, until Massa James could stomach it no more and tried to put a stop to it. When he did, at a moment, Young Massa Roberts turned and struck his brother several times, until Massa James fell hard to the ground. Massa James stood, and, with no words, only an angry look, went to the Big House, gathered his things, and left … not returning for some weeks later.

To no surprise, after Massa James had gone, Young Massa Roberts started his drinking again. I did best to avoid him, although, he kept his manners since Mrs. Lilly was still in the Big House. I begged the Lord, that he wouldn't visit my cabin any night. I guessed the Lord heard, for he didn't come there….

When Massa James returned, he and his brother didn't share many words. Massa James was an easy man with a forgiving soul, so he never spoke about what happened, he just let it go, I guessed.

Word arrived from Mrs. Lilly's sister. She would be coming to fetch Mrs. Lilly in two days. Mrs. Lilly had stayed a few months already, and I was sad that she would be going. I made her a pretty apron, with flowers on it, as a goodbye gift.

Her sister arrived. As she was leaving, and, as I was bending down to hug her, she whispered "One day you'll live as a free woman." Why she said this, I didn't know. We said our goodbyes. A good, kindhearted woman, I was going to miss her awfully.

Now that Mrs. Lilly, had gone the Big House was quieter. Young Massa Roberts and his brother still didn't talk much. Most times, you could grab hold of the tension between them.

One morning, however, Massa James said to his brother, "I'd like to talk business with you." He told Young Massa Roberts that he wanted to bring in paid white servants, three men and one woman. Young Massa Roberts agreed—a miracle, no less. Massa James left on a travel for two days to bring back the servants. I was glad about the woman servant, someone to share my work in the Big House ... a chance to have more time to myself.

While Massa James was away, Young Massa Roberts visited my cabin one night, though—not drunk—different this time. He asked if he could enter. "Yes" was my only answer. It seemed he just wanted to talk, and he did. I had hoped he would leave afterward, but he began taking off his clothes. When it was done, he left. He hadn't hurt me this time, and hadn't made me cry. This was the first time, for a long time, that he had been to my cabin, and I prayed that it would be, just as long for his return.

CHAPTER 9

Massa James returned with the new servants and put them to work. The servant girl was only twenty years in age. She was plump, with long, brown hair, and tall, nearly my height. She spoke softly and was kindly mannered. Her name was Beth, and she called me "Miss Belle," although I told her to call me Belle only—knowing that Young Massa Roberts, would dislike her putting "Miss" before my name. Young Massa Roberts charged me with showing Beth how the Big House ran, now that she would be handling most of the housework.

Beth learned how to do most things in the Big House, meaning I wasn't needed there daily, and Young Massa Roberts paid no notice to my absence. So, I became free to visit the slave quarters and talk to old friends.

One day, when the sun was near fallen, I was visiting the slave quarters and it happened to be one of the older woman's birthday. The slaves celebrated, ate, sang, and danced. I hadn't realized how much I missed being with them since my grandmother's death. Some of the folks remembered me, and my grandmother. They spoke of how I had grown nicely into a woman. In fact, a few men couldn't turn an eye from me, but, because of how I looked, I guessed, none dared to speak much words.

Towards the night's end, one of the men approached me to say hello. His name was Ben. He was thirty-one; he was tall and darkly colored and a single slave man. He said he remembered me, as a young girl living with my grandmother. We talked for a spell. I thought him very nice and figured that I would visit the slave quarters more often, and spend more time with my own kind.

I no longer worked in the Big House every day. I now had time to sew dresses in my cabin, to give to the slave girls, or to trade for things like—fruit, and potatoes, and such. I now knew that I could make a fine living for myself if need be. At times, I dreamed of escaping this plantation and making it on my own.

Early one morning, Young Massa Roberts sent for me to come to the Big House. When I arrived, he said, "You need to work for the next two weeks, because I'll be travelling." And so, he made me head of the servants, paid and slaves, until his return. He said also that Massa James will be there, in charge of the slaves, while he was away—and warned me to keep my distance. I believed that Young Massa Roberts feared his brother learning of all the terrible things he'd done to me, of all the late, night visits to my cabin. One day I would tell Massa James the truth, even if it meant my death.

I was kept to the Big House daily. The servant girl, Beth, was nice and was easy getting along with. She once asked if I were a paid servant. I said no, that I was a slave.

"That's funny," she said, and laughed. I explained that I was born into slavery on this plantation and that I must do always as Massa says. Beth looked at me oddly, then apologized for not understanding.

There were times I felt so mixed up about how I looked, that I didn't look like the other slaves and didn't seem to belong anywhere, not with the slaves nor Massa's people.

One morning, while at work in the Big House, Massa James asked me to talk a bit with him. I had become fearful of our friendship, and he had started to notice.

He asked, "Why have you been so quiet since my return? Is there something I've done to you?"

I had to explaine, that he'd done nothing wrong. "Massa James, you know how your brother can be about you being too friendly with us." Though, I knew that Massa James didn't see me as a slave, but as family, and that I could share anything with him.

He told me not to fear his brother. I said yes—but meant no.

"Besides my brother, you're my closest friend, almost family … like a sister." Chills went up my spine. I said goodbye, then turned and left quickly, to hide my tears.

Afterwards, I headed toward the slave cabin, hoping to see Ben. I liked talking to him—It was nice not having to end each sentence with "Massa". When I saw him, we sat and talked for a long spell, about everything. He asked if I was the daughter of old Massa Roberts, at least that is what was said by most of the slave folks.

"You look white, like old Massa Roberts and his sons, not like the other slaves at all. Guess that's why you work in the Big House, why Massa do so right by you," he said. And just so, the truth began to spill from me: about my true father, and about Young Massa Roberts, how he had treated me for all, of my life.

"I am just a slave, no better than any other slave." I cried into his arms. It felt nice—in fact, near opposite of how I felt around Young Massa Roberts. Ben held me, listened to me, and comforted me warmly.

Now, each day, dusk could not come too soon, so that I could go and see Ben. I had come to care for him dearly and prayed nothing could fall between us.

CHAPTER 10

Even after Young Massa Roberts returned, I was kept in charge of the Big House. After working, most days I would go to see Ben. He'd look at me in a way sometimes, as he wanted to touch me—not to say I would mind—but we dared not, for I feared Young Massa Roberts would kill us if we did … Ben knew this, too. Though, at times, I let him hold my hand and hug me. It felt warm and nice.

My twenty-ninth birthday passed…. Things were alright. I'd come at peace with working in the Big House. Young Massa Roberts and Massa James were getting along well with one another, working nicely together with the plantation, and keeping of the slaves. I still visited the slave quarters to see Ben each day. For once, I felt with my own kind. I only wished to belong somewhere. Though, some of the slave women whispered that I was but trouble for them, and for Ben—and they were probably right. So, I tried best to go carefully about things.

Late, one night, lying in my cabin, I thought of Ben. I hadn't been to the slave quarters in a few days and began to miss him, and sure enough, that night he came knocking at my cabin for the first time. I invited him in—knowing just what he came there for. And just so, I let him have me … so kind and gentle and soft with me. When we finished, he hugged me and left. I had come to love him, and cared not if Young Massa Roberts killed me for it.

Although my times with Ben kept me nervous, we would meet often anyway. We'd find hiding places on the plantation where we would sit and talk, and hug. We talked of being free, of living on our own— though, I didn't wish to live without him. I thought of asking Young Massa Roberts to let us marry. Ben warned, that Young Massa Roberts would likely kill us, and never to say such things. I prayed for us always.

While at work in the Big House one morning, Massa James was looking close at me. "You seem happier now," he said, "something different about you."

Things were all the same, I said in return—lying. And there, I took note of Young Massa Roberts eyeing me sideways—as if he had known something secret of me. I was frightened of what this meant. That night I stayed in my cabin, careful to stay out of Ben's way. I prayed that Ben would not visit that night; something in my stomach warned, that Young Massa Roberts would catch us surely if he did.

And to be sure, later that night, I heard footsteps outside my cabin. It was Young Massa Roberts, bad off with drink— my fears made real. He entered and looked at me for a while, with small eyes and no words.

"Something wrong? Some work you needed me to do?"—I knew the answer.

"Where have you been going each night? I've been coming to your cabin, only to find you gone."

"The women's slave quarters, seeing after some of the ill, and older women," I said.

"You lying to me?" I froze, but, before I answered, he tears my gown off and had his way with me. I was quiet.

When he finished, he looked me cold in the eye and said "You're a fine woman now ... the reason I never took a wife. There is no one I want more so as you, and there will never be another for you, but me. Do right to remember this." He left.

I knew then that Ben and I would never marry, though that would do nothing to stop my love for him. I was Young Massa Robert's sister. What he felt for me was sin. My stomach turned each time he touched me. This had to end. And so, I decided that I would tell Massa James the truth, to ask for his help, in stopping his brother ... Massa James was my only hope now.

Whatever chance I got, while working in the Big House, I started becoming more friendly with Massa James, waiting for the right chance to tell him. I hadn't visited the slave's quarters nor Ben much since Young

Massa Robert's warning. And when I last saw Ben, I told him to stay far from my cabin—though never telling him what Young Massa Roberts had done or said to me that night. Ben—not a fool—agreed.

A lucky morning, while Young Massa Roberts was outside tending to the slaves, I found my chance to sit and talk with Massa James. I told him about my meeting Ben, how we cared for one another dearly, that I wished to marry him.

Massa James smiled and said, "That's wonderful, Belle! I am happy for you." "I see not a reason you and Ben couldn't marry."

"I'll let my brother know this immediately—"

"No!" I said. "I mean … I must tell this to Young Massa Roberts myself." So, Massa James agrees to allow me to tell Young Massa Roberts.

"When you're ready to tell my brother, I be there for you. I'll help you." I thanked him for hearing me well. I felt lighter now that Massa James knew about Ben and I.

The next day, Massa James twenty-ninth birthday came. I had Beth fashion a meal in celebration, and even made a cake myself. Young Massa Roberts joined his brother for the meal. They talked and was drinking peacefully with one another. It was a good night. I was happy for them both. However, I hadn't yet told Ben the good news—that we could marry, that Massa James was happy for us and would help us—and couldn't wait to leave that night.

When I left the Big House, I headed to the slave's quarters and there found Ben. When I arrived most of the slaves were saddened and teary. Turned out, the old slave midwife had passed and everyone was in mourning. I cried, too, as I remembered her helping with the birth of my babies. She would be missed.

Ben told me that she had been sick with fever, and that they would bury her the next day. Afterwards, we just sat silent and held hands for some time.

I then told him of my talk with Massa James, how he was happy for us and agreed to our marriage, but this upset Ben. He said I should have kept quiet about us, that now there would be trouble.

"If Young Massa Roberts finds out, he'd beat me near death for fooling with you," he said. I tried explaining that Massa James was good and kind, and would keep our secret closely. Although Ben became very upset and nervous for us, he then said to me,

"We should stop seeing each other for a spell, and must be careful for now." My heart broke, but I agreed.

CHAPTER 11

It had been nearly two months since I saw Ben, and I missed him greatly.

Then, a morning, while working in the Big House, Young Massa Roberts said, "My brother and I will be leaving for a business trip for three days, and you are to look after things until our return."

"I will look to things very well, Massa" I said. And so, they left.

I couldn't wait until day's end, so that I could visit the slave quarters and see Ben finally.

When I found him, he was glad to see me, much as I was to see him. We talked long. I told him that the Massa's were off on a trip for three days, that we had time to spend together. We went back to my cabin, where he stayed most of the night. I loved Ben much and wished but for us to marry. Only how I would tell Young Massa Roberts without there being trouble, I didn't know. And so, I prayed to Lord.

Young Massa Roberts returned without Massa James, saying that Massa James would arrive in about two days. I just nodded and went about my work.

I feared when Massa James was away. He seemed to be all that could keep Young Massa Roberts off, of me. When I left for my cabin that night, I prayed that Young Massa Roberts would leave me be. He had not been to my cabin in some time.

The next day, while working, I caught attention of Young Massa Roberts staring at me, but when I returned a look, he dropped his head quick and walked away. Maybe he had started to feel wrong for all he had done to me I thought, but could not be sure. I didn't see him again for the rest of that morning. It was a nice morning.

That night, I went to visit Ben. I knew that I should have been more careful since Young Massa Roberts had returned, but I missed him badly. When I found him, he was unhappy about my being there, he told me that I should go about with more care, but we found a place to sit and talk anyway—near a stable that housed the small animals. The moon was full and bright, like a pearl.

Ben felt nervous about me being there, and kept saying I should leave. Finally, I agreed, but, as I stood to leave, someone shouted, "Hey you, over there, stand right now and come here!" Fear caught hold as I saw that it was two of the white men who worked for Young Massa Roberts. I looked to Ben—he looked just as I felt. They yelled for us to come over. We did.

"What were you doing over here?" they asked. I explained that we were only talking. No less, they grabbed Ben and tied his arms behind his back. I screamed that he had done nothing to me.

"We'll send for Young Massa Roberts to see what is to be done with the both of you." I begged them to let Ben go, that we wanted no troubles. They heard nothing, just grabbed and held me, too. I looked at Ben—he wouldn't look back. I started to praying, prayed that Young Massa Roberts doesn't kill us. The men sent a slave to fetch Young Massa Roberts, and then, latched Ben to the whipping post.

Young Massa Roberts arrived, saw me, and asked, "What's going on?"

I told him that Ben and I were only sitting and talking, that we'd done nothing wrong.

"Why were you talking to this man. Is he some kinship?"

I said he is my friend only.

"You will never talk to this man again. He'll be beaten and sold by sunbreak!" I cried out that Ben was my friend, to spare him, and that he'd done no harm to me! Young Massa Roberts slapped me to the ground, and lashed me with the whip. "You have evident of strong feelings for this man, but you'll never see him again. Run off to your cabin, now!"

I ran to my cabin, not looking back. I could hear them beating Ben near to death and wanted to die with him. I hoped that Young Massa Roberts would come and kill me, too, for I had no wish to live without Ben. I cried. I stopped my prayers—wasn't sure if I'd ever been heard. When I came to my cabin, my mind looked to ways to kill myself ... until I just fell to the floor and cried.

Young Massa Roberts came in. "You will never go to the slave's quarters again. Hear me!" "There is no one for you but me, and I'll beat this into you if need be."—He did—and then I felt what my mother felt. He left, and I just lay on the floor, only wishing to die.

CHAPTER 12

How long I lay that way on the floor, I didn't know....

Someone knocked to my cabin door, and startled me up. It was one of the slave girls from the Big House. She'd been sent to wash me and to see that I ate some food. I had no reply—and no care anymore. She cleaned me and helped me to my cot. She tried to get me to eat. I didn't. She stayed until night came, then left. The next day was a repeat: the slave girl returned, cleaned me, tried to feed me, but couldn't.

Sickness was starting on me, and I was thinner—but still only cared for dying. The girl said that she would come—had to come—each day and help me until I was stronger. I said nothing.

Each day, she would brush my hair and talk to me—but I never heard her—and when night came she would leave. Days passed, but I stayed the same. I was dying, I knew it, I welcomed it.

One morning, I heard the slave girl outside the cabin, only it wasn't her that entered, but Massa James.

"Belle, I learned what happened and am terribly sorry." "I am the one who sent the slave girl to look after you. She says you won't eat. Belle, I need you to get stronger. There is something I wish to talk of, with you— something planned that will require your strength. Belle, don't die—not if you want to be a free woman."

I turned my head to him but said nothing still. As he left, he said that he would keep the slave girl tending to me until I was better.

"Okay," I whispered.

Months passed and I stayed in my cabin still, but my health had begun to return. I had not been to the Big House for some time now, yet Young

Massa Roberts did nothing and had not returned to my cabin since *that* night.

Each time I thought of Ben, I cried, and cried because I would never see him again. I am thirty years in age and now knew that I would never marry…. I prayed always, asking the Lord to rid my heart of the hatred of Young Massa Roberts.

Through the slave girl, Massa James had given me stacks of notes and books, and told me I must learn to speak and act properly—like a free woman. I didn't understand what he had planned, but it gave me hope to go on. Massa James said he would explain his plans more later.

I felt that it was time to tell Massa James the truth, about what his daddy said and my promise to him, how Young Massa Roberts had treated me for too long. Massa James needed to know, all of it, even if his brother killed me for it.

One morning, Massa James came to my cabin to talk. By then, I was far better, nearly back to myself. Massa James smiled and said that he was happy to see me well again. I thanked him for his help and the slave girl he'd sent to see after me. He told me that Young Massa Roberts was off on a trip for the day and would not return until the next morning, meaning we could talk without worry.

I told him everything … about the night his daddy died, about the promise. He believed me.

"No wonder you've never looked like the other slaves," he said.

I told of how Young Massa Roberts had treated me all my life, that even when I told Young Massa Roberts what his father had said, that I was his sister, he never accepted it, saying rather that I was just his property to do with as he pleased. Massa James sat quiet with tears in his eyes.

"Worry no more, Belle. I plan to take you from here—far—somewhere you can live out the rest of your life freely." He wanted to take me to new lands and for me to meet new people, wanted to treat me as a sister. Because of how I looked, I would play the role of his *white* sister, which was why I had to learn to speak and act as a proper free woman.

"I'll take you from here, and we'll never return," he said. I cried and thanked Massa James for believing me and accepting me as his sister. I agreed to learn whatever he wished me to. He had given me hope, and for that, I was grateful.

When he returned, and learned that I was again well, Young Massa Roberts sent for me to return to work at the Big House. The servant girl, Beth, had gone off to be married, and so again, I was charged with all the running of the Big House. I paid no mind since it gave me more chance to see and talk with Massa James.

He gave me books that would teach me of lands and places that I should know of before we escaped. He said we would cross many lands, to get to a boat that would take us far across the waters. I was learning also how to dress and speak as a proper lady, how to walk. He told me to no longer call him Massa, that he was my brother, and such, that we would travel as brother and sister. My mind ran always with these thoughts and excitements, until I could no longer sleep at night.

Once, while in the Big House, speaking with Massa James, his brother entered and overheard me.

"You're talking far better, guess it's those books you read always, huh?" I just nodded my head and left as quickly as I could, and thanked the Lord that he had not caught on to why I was speaking better.

CHAPTER 13

Months passed as I continued to read and learn more. Massa James had me sew several dresses for myself—eight in all—said I must have changes of clothes to wear for when we took off. Massa James also sent a slave girl to my cabin with a package—a cloak and a pair of women's shoes. I was told to hide them until we took off. Every day, I prayed that nothing would stop our escape and thanked the Lord for allowing me this chance at a better life. I often had to try well, to hide my joy from Young Massa Roberts.

One afternoon, Massa James told me that he would be taking a trip, returning with a new paid servant girl, and to settle some things for our travels. The new servant girl would take charge of my usual work in the Big House. When he said, he would be gone four days, I could not hide my tears. I was fearful of what Young Massa Roberts might do while he was away— and Massa James knew this.

"Belle, be strong. Hold on and know that you are almost free, but I must leave to arrange everything." I agreed to be strong—though fear still in my heart—then said goodbye for the time.

After two days, Young Massa Roberts called to me and said to be sure I taught the new servant girl the workings of the Big House well, when she arrived. I said yes, but I knew there was more to it.

Then, he said, "I'll be *visiting* you tonight to discuss something"—a strike to my heart. It had been so long, and I was unsure whether I had the spirit to bear *it* again. That day, after leaving the Big House, I hurried to my cabin to hide the things I had gathered for our travels.

That evening, Young Massa Roberts came as promised.

"Things look different here … nicer," he said. He sat and talked of how I had become a proper lady, and how he would love to invite me on one of his in-town travels. I tried hard to put away my hatred. He said he'd even thought of moving me into the Big House.

I wanted nothing more than for Massa James and I to leave right away, or else, die, than to suffer any of these things with Young Massa Roberts. Then, as feared, he grabbed me and had me … though kindly and gently. Maybe, he had a twisted way of loving me, but, no less, I was his sister and would never return that love. I prayed that was the last time.

Massa James returned with the new white servant girl, Nora, a pretty and kind girl, twenty-five years in age. Over a few months, I showed Nora how to do everything in the Big House, though she was a bit slow learning things. But, given time, Nora understood all the workings.

Nora seemed to fancy Young Massa Roberts, and he was kind with her always. This joyed me to see, hoping that Young Massa Roberts would actually find, a woman—besides me—maybe a wife even. As time marched on, Young Massa Roberts spent more attention on Nora, them talking more and often.

Turned out, this is just what Massa James wanted to happen—wise— to give Young Massa Roberts a distraction from me. It worked well because Young Massa Roberts no longer paid me much mind—and I was thankful for it. Massa James and I could now talk freely and settle our plans to leave.

While working with Nora, I would often pay attention to her manners, how she spoke, and how she acted, to study closely the ladylike mannerisms of a free white woman, and, each evening, in my cabin, I would practice and mock what I had learned—like how to walk proper in women's shoes. Massa James said these were the things I must learn before we could leave, that I could no longer speak—not even think—as a negro slave. To learn of the places, we would travel to, Massa James gave me books, and for writing, about my life and our travels, he gave me paper plenty. I had learned of the land we lived: Alabama. And learned of England, the country Massa James said we would travel to, where we would live out our remaining days.

Massa James said he had friends that would help us along the way. He was a smart man, even had a natural taste for business—unlike his brother, who nearly lost the plantation. Massa James said that when we landed in England, we would open a bakery and that I could make and sell dresses. That sounded nice. There was a mixed of feelings in my stomach: fright, nervousness, and, more than all else, happiness.

CHAPTER 14

Once, while at work with Nora, she asked whether I was Young Massa Robert's sister—just as he walked in.

"She's a slave," he answered "and I forbid you from ever saying otherwise in this house again!" Terror—and tears—filled her eyes, as she apologized a hundred times over. Young Massa Roberts sent her outside for a breath, until she had calmed. When she had gone, he turned and slapped me hard to the floor.

"You'll have no more conversations with Miss Nora, unless absolutely necessary. Hear me?" I did.

When he had gone, I climbed to a chair and thought, of how I had never fit with the slaves—because I looked white—and how I had never fit with Young Massa Roberts because I was a slave. I did not know what freedom could offer me, but I prayed for it no less.

Massa James said that the preparations were but settled, though, we had not been able to talk much, with Young Massa Roberts always being around. So, a day, when Young Massa Roberts had gone into town on business, Massa James and I found moments to talk.

Massa James said the trip had been set. He had papers that said I was born to his Father, that I was his sister and that my name was Belle Roberts. He made my birthday one year sooner than his own. I must remember this and keep the papers on me always. So, it seemed, escaping the plantation would no longer be a dream only. It had become real.

I was so happy, yet terrified always. I had gone no farther than the plantation my entire life, and when we escaped, we could never return. That was why Massa James gave me writing paper, to put to word my life and memories, that I should write of my life on the plantation and

41

afterwards, of our travels. So, some nights, I would sit in my cabin and write of the day's happenings.

By then, I had learned to read, speak, write, and walk as well as any white woman. I had learned of a wide world was beyond this plantation, and was blessed in that I would see it soon.

I reached my thirty-first birthday. My mind was full with all that was happening, so I didn't give much care to it, but Massa James no less had one of the girls, fashion me a small cake. He sent her to my cabin with the cake and a note that read, "Enjoy your last birthday on the plantation." I cried with joy.

Late one night, I was waked by screams; coming from near the slave quarters, I wondered as to what had happened. Turned out, the white workers had caught two young slave boys trying to escape. They had beat them bloody. They sent for Young Massa Roberts, on how they should further handle the boys. The boys were fourteen and sixteen, and they were brothers.

Young Massa Roberts arrived, learned what had happened and ordered, "Hang them, and be sure the other slaves watch, to learn what happens to runners."

"They are but boys. Wasn't the beating enough? These boys aren't animals. Don't slaughter them as such," said Massa James.

We all cried and begged for the boys' lives. Young Massa Roberts hanged them still. Massa James screamed at his brother, that, one day, he would leave him and never return.

Young Massa Roberts said, "These are my lands, my slaves, and my property to do with as it please me. Our Father left all this to *me*, and such, things will be run as I see fit! My brother, you'd do well to respect and remember that."

That night, I prayed long for those boys and their families. I began wondering of all the slaves I would leave behind, of how their suffering would not stop with my escape, and prayed even harder, for their mercy.

Massa James's thirty-first birthday came as well. That day, he was leaving to visit Mrs. Lilly, his wife's mother, for some days. He told me not to worry—as I already was—that everything was in place. He said to stay strong and that he promised not to leave me long with his brother. And so, he left.

The next day, I caught sound of Nora crying in the kitchen. I did not talk to her much after what Young Massa Roberts had said, but, for the moment, he was outside on the plantation. I asked why she was crying.

"I am with child," she said—I was with shock. "My mother has died and I have only my father. He'd be terribly upset if he found out I was pregnant but unmarried."

"Who be the child's father?" I asked. I fainted nearly, when she said that is was Young Massa Roberts. "Does he know?" I asked.

She said no, that she was afraid to tell him. She had to, I told her, to see how he felt about it. I hoped maybe this would be the needed change for Young Massa Roberts, that he might take Nora as his wife. I could only pray for her and her child for now.

When Massa James returned, I told him of the child, that it was his brother's. After talking with Massa James, Nora decided on telling Massa Roberts about the baby. Though she begged Massa James not to say anything, that she would rather wait until the chance to tell him herself.

Several days passed before Miss Nora told Young Massa Roberts about the child. And to everyone's surprise, Young Massa Roberts accepted the news of the baby readily, and agreed to marry Nora. I was happy for Nora and her baby—and myself. I knew that I could now leave without concern for Young Massa Roberts; that now, that he had a family to hold his attention, I would not be missed.

The Big House was in a fuss about Miss Nora and Young Massa Roberts's marriage ceremony, that would take place on the plantation grounds. Young Massa Roberts even sent for her Father.

CHAPTER 15

Several months had gone since Young Massa Roberts and Mrs. Nora's marriage. Mistress Nora was now full with child, and was no longer able to work in the Big House, and so, charge fell back to me. Massa James had been trying hard to sell the thought to Young Massa Roberts that a new servant was necessary, to help with the house and Mistress Nora—and to make my leaving easier on Young Massa Roberts. Young Massa Roberts agreed finally. In accord, he then left for near a week to find a new servant.

He returned with an older white woman. Her name was Mrs. Anna; she was thirty-nine years in age. She was well learned in most work, and a swift study. She had the running of Big House down in a short time. She proved stern with the slave women, also—this, Young Mass Roberts liked. He also made sure she did not mistake me as anything but a slave, and so her sternness spread to me, too.

Massa James kept me calm, reminding me always that I would be free soon, but, as our escape became closer, I became more nervous.

One night, Young Massa Roberts entered my cabin, said he *needed* me now, that his wife, too full with child, and could not tolerate relations. So, he had me ... though, during, he apologized often.

"I won't hurt you, Belle. I'll be gentle. Though, don't lose mind that this is your purpose, to please me as needed," he said.

I squeezed my eyes shut and pretended that I was somewhere else, that I was free, living in far new lands.

When he'd finished, he said "I will come again, until my wife is able to receive me."

When he had gone, I cried to the Lord to let Mistress Nora's baby be born and she be healed as quick as could be—for his focus to turn back to his wife.

The time had come for Mistress Nora's baby to be born. Lucky, Mrs. Anna was skilled in midwifery. She and I both guided Mistress Nora in her baby's birth, while Young Massa Roberts and Massa James awaited news outside.

It was a baby boy, strong, healthy, and well. Young Massa Roberts was overjoyed at the news. He named him John Roberts III, after his own father. Massa James was also very happy for his brother ... but, in that moment, I could think only of my two dead children, fathered by Young Massa Roberts, and how I could never have another child of my own, nor raise one up as my own—and so, no happiness was shared by me that day.

It was Young Massa Roberts's thirty-six, birthday and there were preparations all about for his celebration. Mistress Nora and Mrs. Anna were in a fuss, setting up the Big House for the invited guests. Everyone was quite busy, which gave Massa James and I a chance to talk.

"Belle, pack away your belongings. I'll be sending someone to your cabin to retrieve them. I have a wagon hidden on the lands where they'll be stored."

My heart missed beats. I had near lost my nerve.

"Everything will be perfectly alright," he said, catching the emotion in my face. "We'll talk more later."

I had no words for this, nor for the rest of the day.

Two days later, there was a knock at my cabin door: two slaves, a woman and man, had come to fetch my belongings to be put into the wagon. They seemed to believe that all the belongings I was handing off to them, were to be given away—supposed they were told that by Massa James, not foolish enough to spill our true plans. I gave them all that I had packed and off they went into the night. That night I got no sleep.

Young Massa Roberts, too happy with his family, and paid me no attention anymore. He even seemed kinder to the slave women that worked in the Big House. He had not come to my cabin since Mistress Nora had recovered—God bless it. He longer even minded my talks with his brother.

With Young Massa Roberts distracted, I felt as if this was really, going to happen, that I'd be free finally.

Young Massa Roberts would be off soon on a business trip for a handful of days, said Massa James, and that is when we would head off. That night I prayed for strength—I would need it more than ever.

The time arrived for Young Massa Roberts to leave for his trip. Mistress Nora gave him a list of things to fetch for her and the baby while he was in town.

"Belle, you and Mrs. Anna are to look after the house and my family while I'm away, and James will look to the lands and fields." I agreed happily—knowing that this was goodbye forever. I would be a lie to say I did not feel a little sad. That plantation and its slaves were all I had ever known as home, and family. Young Massa Roberts caught the look on my face, and asked if I could handle things. I nodded yes.

Massa James visited my cabin that night. We talked of the trip and he said that he had the wagon all packed, that we would leave tomorrow. He had the slave women pack food and water plenty, and he said that we would takes two good horses to hitch to the wagon. He said that it would two, maybe three days to arrive at our first stop, a place where he had friends that would help us and that we would be able to rest.

"And be sure to no longer call me Master—just James. You won't be a slave. You'll be my sister. Note this well."

The next morning, Massa James told Mrs. Anna that he would be taking a trip in-town, to buy feed and supplies for the livestock, and that I would be coming along to help, and to be sure to take care of things while we were away. Mrs. Anna agreed—though with a suspect look to her face.

We left at dusk. I said goodbye to no one, as to give the appearance of my eventual return. As we rode off, Massa James smiled at me.

"You are now a free woman, Belle," he said.

And so, we left—never looking back.

CHAPTER 16

When had been travelling a day, when I started to cry suddenly. My brother, James, asked why was I crying? I told him that even if we never made it to where we were headed, that I thanked him—and the Lord—still for all that he had done, that I was thankful to be free and that I will make him proud, wherever we went. He hugged me and smiled. I knew I didn't have to worry about James hurting me, for he truly treated me as his sister.

We stopped for the night to rest. When daylight came, I awoke and fetched us some water to splash our faces. Then, we continued. We had yet some traveling still, before we came unto the first town. Try not as I did, I stopped and stared at this new world in wonder, when we arrived there.

"Please do better not to act so surprised. Act normal, as if you've seen such things before," James warned.

So, I did my best to not speak or stare much, until I had gotten a bit more used to it all—the houses, shops, buildings, and people going about. We were headed to a house belonging to a friend of James—just beyond the town—our first rest stop.

We arrived at a large house, the home of Mr. Williams and his wife Mrs. Debra Mae, James said. They welcomed us in without question and Mrs. Debra Mae showed me to my room.

"I'll send up a slave girl with water so that you can freshen up," she said.

When she left, I looked around the room and felt out of place. There was a bed with pillows and pretty coverings. I had never slept in a bed and I did not know what to feel about it, but, no less, I would play along. I realized that this would take some time to get used to—to play the part of a free, white woman, to no longer be a negro slave.

The slave girl entered my room with a wash basin and water, and asked if I needed help. "No," I said and thought to myself that I would not dare let a slave fuss over me, remembering that I had been a slave but days ago; for I knew what that was like.

After we had bathed and rested, Mr. Williams and his wife sent for James and I to join them for supper. I was terrified, that I could not play the proper way, as a free white woman.

"Just remain calm, and think before you speak. If you are unsure of something, just smile and nod," James told me.

I trusted him and did as he said. The dinner went well, and the Williamses proved to be very nice people. They were even polite with their slaves, saying "please" and "thank you" to them always.

James said we would stay a few days, then, afterwards, we would be off again. —That night, I found I quite liked sleeping in a real bed. The next morning, James and Mr. Williams went into town to buy supplies. While they were away, Mrs. Debra Mae asked me to lunch with her, on the front porch—which seemed to wrap full around the house. The slaves served us our meal. We ate salads, warmed rolls, and drank tea, still so much for me to take in. Not ever being served by anyone.

"How old are you, and why have you not married yet?" she asked. "You are too fine a young woman to not have found a husband yet."

I explained that I had to care for my father while he was ill, and, when he passed, I helped looked after his home with my brother—all half-truths, but she seemed to believe them. In fact, Mrs. Debra Mae never seemed to see me, as anything other than a white woman, which gave me the confidence that I could truly pull this off.

James and Mr. Williams returned, sat, and shared a drink in the sitting room. Mr. Williams told James of roads to take, other than those he had mapped out, while we travelled. On these roads, he said, we would not run into any slave bounty hunters. He said they caused troubles for anyone that passed their way and to go about carefully. Mr. Williams said they looked for runaway slaves to return to their masters for payment. And if they could not get payed, then they settled with killing the slaves. I could only pray that we would never see these men.

Time came for us to leave. We said our goodbyes and thanked them for everything. As we were heading off, Mrs. Debra Mae stopped me and gave me a bonnet to wear on my head,

she said, "This'll keep out the winds and sunlight from your face while you travel."

I hugged and thanked her again for their kindness. The Williamses had few slaves on their lands ... all of it, in fact, was so different. Their slaves wore shoes, lived in nicer cabins, and did not work in fields, only in gardens and in the house. The Williamses were simple folks, nice folks. I had never known that there were white people like them; however, James said, that most of the friends of his I would meet were like the Williams— that not everyone was like his brother.

CHAPTER 17

We were back on the road. James said that it would be several days before we reached the next town. We would be staying in a place called an inn, he said, where we could pay for rooming.

We arrived at the next town, and it was bigger even than the last one—with many buildings, shops, houses, drinking places, and more white people than I have ever seen. I feared that someone would discover me as a negro slave. James told me to be sure I kept on my bonnet and to remain silent. My stomach churned. He said he would check us into the inn, where I could then rest easy.

When we came to the inn, James paid for two rooms. The man behind the desk paid me no mind—which did well to ease my fear. James said that we would be a few days only, as to allow the horses—and ourselves—time to rest.

Later, when we had settled into our rooms, James said, "I'm going out to get some food and water. Remain in the room until I return." He then handed me his satchel, which held the money and other important papers. He told me to keep it until he returned and that he would do this each time he left; so, that in case something happened to him, I would have all I needed to continue the trip—which only made me pray for his safe return after he had gone.

He returned with enough food to last a handful of days, enough, at least, to last our stay at the inn. We talked much and often during our stay. James explained that we must put a distance between us and Young Massa Roberts, for, by now, he had learned of our escape surely, and most likely had sent men after us. He said we must keep moving, stopping only with people he trusted—and who did not know his brother.

He said that there would be things I would see along the way, that I must show no emotion towards. There were white people, he said, who would beat or kill not only runaway slaves, but anybody that attempted to help them, and that I must take care to keep quiet about whatever I saw happen to slaves.

I was happy to leave that town, to leave all those white people—some who I thought I had seen staring at me sideways. Our next stop would be a plantation owned by friends of James: Mr. Raymond, his wife, and his two children. James warned that they had many slaves on their plantation, which meant I would have to control my emotions, that I would have to wear my best acting face. To appear better off, James had us stop, clean up, and put on new changes of clothes.

When we arrived, the Raymond plantation was huge and beautiful, the house itself, wrapped with flower gardens and having a wide front porch, with benches on each end and decorated with baskets of more flowers. In fact, the flowers perfumed the entire plantation.

The Raymond family met us on the front porch. They seemed friendly and welcomed us into their home. Introductions were made. His wife's name was Mrs. Ruth, and their two children were Willie Raymond Jr, and Sallie—nine and ten years old. They showed us around inside and, then, to our rooms, so that we could clean up and rest a bit.

Mrs. Ruth's kindness helped put my nerves at ease, and she seemed to suspect nothing of me, only that I was James's sister. They later invited us for supper in the parlor. The Raymond's had prepared a feast for our arrival. The meal was nice and full with talk. I thought that I would not mind living this way always—slavery aside.

"Are you married?" asked Mrs. Ruth.

I said that I was not. Hearing that, she wanted me to meet her brother, who would be coming the next day for dinner. I agreed nervously. She said her brother's name was Mr. Johnathon and that he was two years older than I was.

After supper, Mrs. Ruth had a slave girl show me back to my room, where she was to assist me with getting ready for bed. I allowed her to help me, but I did so kindly as possible. It was so strange to hear her put "miss" repeatedly before my name. I disliked it, but said nothing, only thanked her as she left.

The next morning, Mrs. Ruth had me join her in the breakfast room. It was bright and large, with a big round, table that could host six people. The room was wrapped in tall windows that let in the sunlight without charge, with flowers hung everywhere—guessed Mrs. Ruth quite fancied them. When I came down, her children were already eating breakfast. There was food aplenty, iced tea, and a handful of different juices all being served. Her slave women servants, neatly wore white aprons atop grey dresses. Mrs. Ruth was not mean to them—but kept a stern voice.

While eating, Mrs. Ruth asked, "What do you use on your skin to keep such a pretty glow?"

Nothing but the sun from our travels, I lied.

"Well, you are very pretty, and I would love for you to meet my brother Johnathan."

All the men returned and we decided to rest on the front porch, while her children played in the lands. I saw that the cotton fields stretched far back on the plantation and that the Raymond's had many slaves working in them.

"My family owns near two hundred slaves. In fact, we are one of the largest cotton plantations in this area. This is how we make our wealth … The secret" she said "is to keep the slaves healthy and well, fed. That way they can work harder and longer. There is great profit in it, darling"

I listened and nodded only, for I knew nothing of the facts she spoke of. Then made quick note of her beautiful flower gardens and home. She enjoyed the perfume of flowers, she said, that was why she put them all about the house.

When evening came, Mr. Raymond, James, and Mrs. Ruth's brother, Mr. Johnathan, who arrived for dinner as promised, all cleaned up for supper. Mr. Johnathan was a tall man with the bluest eyes—though a not-so-friendly smile. My brother James shot me a glance— "I don't trust him," his eyes warned. During supper, Mr. Johnathon asked, "Where exactly are you and your brother headed?"

Before I could speak, "I am taking my sister to a school, where she'll learn to be a teacher," James interrupted.

I smiled, and nodded.

"And are you unmarried?" he asked.

I said that was true, and then fed them the same half-truths I had given to Mrs. Debra Mae. James smiled then.

Afterwards, everyone went into the sitting room, the men for drinks and the women for tea, where Mr. Johnathon commented on how handsome a woman I was, and said that he hoped we would meet again someday. I thanked him nicely, then excused myself to my bedroom just as nicely. I slept peacefully knowing, that when morning had fallen, we would be leaving this place—and that man.

CHAPTER 18

After leaving the Raymond's plantation, we traveled for a few days. One night, James decided that we should rest near the river—for the horses to drink. As we got closer to the river, I caught glimpse of lights in the forest; James saw them, too. We decided to see just what they were. When we had gotten to a point, we saw that the light was from torches—torches held in hand by a group of men. My stomach knotted. James warned me to keep quiet and put on my bonnet, that he would manage the talking.

When they saw us, they asked where we were heading? "I am taking my sister off to be schooled," James said.

One of the men held out the light closer to me as to get a firmer look. "Evening, mam," he said.

I squeezed a smile and nodded back.

Afterwards, they waved to James and I, that we had best get on and they let us go by. That was when my eyes saw four slave men, and two women, hanging dead from a tree. My breath caught, but James looked fast to me— as to show no feelings. The men then started cutting down and burning the bodies.

And there, standing amidst these horrible men burning the bodies, was Mr. Johnathon. His eye caught me, and he tipped his hat and smiled, though I could not return the gesture. It hurt my heart to see what my people had to suffer, and yet show no emotions of outward grief. When out of sight of the men, I began to pray for those souls, and their loved ones, with tears running down my face.

"Those were slave bounty hunters. They collect money by returning runaway slaves to their masters. And if the slaves can't be returned or no money can be collected, well—you saw", my brother replied.

James said that he thought it evil what those men did, that slaves were no less human and did not deserve to be treated like cattle. He said that we could not stop until we were well clear of those bounty hunters, and so we kept on. We would soon be reaching the home of a family, who helped runaway slaves, he said, and that was likely, where the slaves that the bounty hunters had captured, were headed. There we would rest a few days. He said that they were very kind people who knew that I was a slave already.

As we travelled, I had written about all that I had seen, but James explained that I could not write about the people we would be meeting. Since they aided runaway slaves, he wanted to be sure that I left no record of them, a record that could fall in unfriendly hands. I agreed that I would not speak of their home's location nor appearance.

"These are good, kind-hearted, God-fearing people, and no one can know of what they did"

I had never known of such white people and thanked the Lord for them.

We stayed a few days while James traded our horses for younger ones. We freshen up and got new supplies, then continued, on our way.

James said, "We must put a great distance between my brother and us. I don't believe he would still be searching for us, but, if he is, we won't be found, in the south nor the north. I've paid for two passages on a boat to England. There, my brother would never find us."

There, he said, we would live out our years in peace. I knew little about England, only that we had to cross far waters to reach it. I had seen the way my people suffered, in many lands, and did not know what to expect. I had learned that Ill treatment of the negro slaves was not just on the plantation, from which I had escaped. I no longer thought of how Young Massa Roberts had treated me, for I had now seen far worse. I wondered that if I were born not looking as I do, would any of this be possible still, would James have ever planned this escape for me as he did. My opportunity allowed me to see what most could not, through the eyes of a negro slave women, yet walking free in white skin.

We had travelled more than a month, and had crossed through many towns and lands new to me. I had yet to be questioned as anything but a white woman, which gave me the courage to act and move about more freely.

We arrived at yet another rest place. The home of a rancher, my brother said. His home was a lovely cattle and horse ranch. His name was Mr. Dean. Mr. Dean had two daughters, named Miss Shelly and Young Amy, who he raised alone, since their mother had died long ago. They welcomed us to their home kindheartedly.

They had but a few slaves that tended to the land and animals. They also had paid white servants. The house was run by an older servant woman named Mrs. Donna, who showed us to our rooms. James said we would rest here four days. I quite liked this place—liked its quiet, peace, and beauty.

Young Amy later came and fetched us for dinner. Young Amy was fourteen and her sister, Miss Shelly, was twenty. During supper, Miss. Shelly told us that she was being schooled to become a nurse. Though, all while she spoke, Miss. Shelly could not take an eye away from James, but he seemed not to notice. She was a pretty, young lady, tall with long, yellow curly hair, and bright blue eyes. My brother had aged and looked worn with the stress of his travels, and now possessed a rugged handsomeness. Although his looks were most from his mother, he had his father's eyes, and he was tall—like me. Miss. Shelly continued to talk, passing, now and then, a shy look to James. I never thought of my brother as a widower, and never thought, that he would marry again someday.

When the supper ended, Mr. Dean asked James if they could speak privately—though, how he said it made me worry. Later, James came to my room and said that Mr. Dean had shown him a "Wanted" note that had spread through a number, of towns. It described James's appearance and my own, and tagged me a runaway slave. Young Massa Roberts was offering a large bounty to anyone who arrested James, and returned me as his property. My heart dropped into my stomach. James said that if the letter had reached this far, our time here would have to be cut to two days.

"Mr. Dean was only warning us. He has no intention of turning us into the authorities," he explained.

Sleep did not come that night.

During breakfast the next morning, Mr. Dean could not turn his eyes from me, as if he disbelieved that I was a negro slave. I felt ill, and no longer comfortable sleeping in their beds or sitting at their table. Though, they treated me no differently. It seemed, that Mr. Dean had not told any of his people about our secret.

After breakfast, Mr. Dean gave James the tour of his lands, and afterwards, took him into town to purchase more supplies for our trip. Miss Shelly invited me to sit with her and her sister outside for a time. It was warm out, the sun beating down brightly, though they had a covering atop the table to shade us. Lovely flowers were planted all about, so peaceful and beautiful.

As we sat and drank sweet tea with ice chips, Miss Shelly asked me if my brother James was married. I told her that his wife had died. And she asked me what kind of work I did? I said that I was also going to school to be a teacher, and explained, that was the reason for our travels. She wanted to know why I had not yet married. I had not met anyone, I replied. Miss Shelly said that I was very pretty and that it should not be hard for me to find a husband. I just smiled. All the time, I watched for Mr. Dean's return, for I felt that he would dislike a slave talking with his daughter so. Before Mr. Dean could catch us, I made an excuse to leave that sunny place and headed back to my room for the day.

I didn't come down for supper when I was sent for. Instead, I had my meal brought to my room, as to avoid Mr. Dean's watchful eyes—which also gave Miss Shelly time alone with my brother.

In the dead of night, when the house was asleep, I heard my room door open. I thought it was one of the girls or James. It was Mr. Dean.

"You know what I want, don't you?" he said. I nodded my head.

I let the tears flow and said yes.

"Now I know you're a runaway slave—and I know you're not pure, either. Do just as I say and be sure to keep quiet, and you'll have no problems with me turning in you and your brother. Understand?"

And once again, as he had me through the night, I was at the mercy, of the white man's nature. The next morning, I cleaned myself up long and hard. I forced through breakfast with Mr. Dean and his daughters. When breakfast had finished, Miss Shelly packed us food and supplies for the road. We hugged, said our goodbyes, and headed off—the whole time, Mr. Dean wearing a grin on his face.

I never told James about that night. And, as we travelled, James caught attention of my silence and asked if everything was fine. I said no, that I had become weary with travel and was longed for a place to call home. James understood and wanted just the same thing—but our travels were not done, we had yet some distance to go.

CHAPTER 19

We came to another town—small, dotted with only a few buildings and shops—where James decided we would check into an inn and rest.

After I had settled a bit, he asked me to join him as he shopped for new supplies. As we walked, I noticed that there were few people on the streets. No one seemed to notice me nor James. Though, I felt uneasy, knowing that Young Massa Roberts was on the hunt still for us. We had no clue how far and to whom those wanted posters had spread, only that we must keep moving. "The farther north we go, the harder it will be for my brother to find us," James said.

We would travel until we arrived at the boat that would take us to England. I had never seen an ocean, nor knew of it until I read about it in the books James had given me. Now, Lord bless, I had been given the chance to not only see one, but cross one.

We had travelled near three months and come yet to another town—a big one. People went all about, riding on horses and wagons. Shop stalls owned the streets, each busy with people trading their wares.

"We are nearly out of the south— a bit farther and we needn't worry about my brother anymore," James said of the town. He said we were only passing through, that we would be staying with friends of his wife's family who lived just outside of town. We would stay a week, he said. He warned that they lived on a plantation, not unlike the one we had come, with many slaves and that I must take care to control my nerves.

At town's edge, we came upon a large group of white men, crowded around a raised platform. On the platform, there were slave men and women being prodded like cattle. James explained that this was a slave auction, where slaves were bought and sold. Seeing that, I realized just how shameful it was to pretend to be one of these people. That I had to look like them, walk like them, and talk like them, all in order, to be free of them.

We reached the home of the Joneses, the family friends of James's passed wife, where we would make our stay. Atop the main gates, there was a sign that read "Welcome to the Joneses' Homestead." It reminded me much of James's family plantation—with a wide land and lots of slaves at work in the fields and farming the land, with a big house and small slave cabins laid far back on the lands. The likeness of it all undid my nerves.

Mr. Jones, and his wife were older people, his wife was very ill and bedridden. Their daughter, Mrs. Ruby, and her husband, Mr. Ron lived with them, also. Mrs. Ruby and Mr. Ron looked after the main bit of the house and plantation for their parents. They led us to our rooms and told us when supper would be ready.

On the way to supper, I notice the inside of the house. It was large with a number, of rooms. They had negro slave women who were fussing about, cleaning, cooking, and serving them. Slave women bounced back and forth from Mrs. Jones's room—the ill wife— tending to each of her needs. The house was alive with movement.

When I entered the parlor for supper, only Mrs. Ruby sat there. She had me sit with her and eat. As we ate, she proved polite, treating me as well as she would treat herself.

She told me, "The men eat their meals before the women always. Now they're plopped down in the sitting room, talking business."

It calmed me to know, that there would be some separation between the men and me—as to avoid a repeat of what happened with Mr. Dean.

Mrs. Ruby told me that her mother had seventy years to her name and was in bad health. Because of this, she said, I would be unable to meet her. "But feel free to walk about the place. There are sitting benches all about. The one I like in particular is right on the bank of the small pond. You'll find it quite peaceful."

I said that perhaps the next day, I would look about.

I saw James none that day. And I returned to my room and rested until the morning. I was awakened early by a young slave girl—maybe of ten years—who undid the draperies to allow in the sunlight. She gave me fresh water to wash with and asked if I needed help getting dressed. I said no, and thanked her. She told me that breakfast would be outside that morning and that Mrs. Ruby would await me. I got dressed and allowed the slave girl to lead me out to where breakfast was held.

It was right out the back of the house, a nice space, with a large round table and chairs, ringed with flowers, and with a wide view of the pond where you could see ducks swimming—so peaceful, as Mrs. Ruby promised.

As I joined her at the table, the slave women brought out breakfast on rolling carts, stocked fully with many kinds of food, and juices, and teas. Again, the men did not join us.

Mrs. Ruby said that the men had their breakfast earlier and were now out on the lands. Mrs. Ruby was twenty-eight years, her husband thirty-two. She told me she was with child—but too early to show still. She said how she so loved to come out there in the morning and take in the fresh air. She had a gentle spirit and spoke very softly to me and the slaves, too.

During breakfast, James and Mrs. Ruby's husband appeared and joined us. We shared good morning's and Mr. Ron bent down and sat a kiss on his wife's forehead. They said they would be going to town and would be back before supper.

Later that day, I returned to the pond and sat down on one of the benches, warmed by the high sun. I could see the slaves at work in the fields, and could even hear some of them singing.

While sitting, I had begun to write in my journal when I heard the trot of horses. I raised my head and saw two negro slave men walking my way, with horses in hand. I felt nervous and lowered my head, trying best to neither look nor speak to them. As they passed, they said good evening madam. When I looked up to return the greeting, one of men, for a moment, seemed stopped by what he saw, but then dropped his head quickly, and continued walking. But I had already seen him—It was ben!

I shouted out his name, but he turned back to me, stopped, then said, "There be no one by the name of Ben here, mam." Then he went on.

I sat and watched after them until they escape my sight. I then ran back to my room and cried myself to sleep—for it was truly my Ben… And it pained me most that I could not do, nor say a thing about it. I felt sick at heart the rest of the day. When Mrs. Ruby sent for me to come for supper, I did not join her; so, Mrs. Ruby sent a slave girl up to my room with food, and a message, that she hoped that I got better. I knew that I must tell James about this as soon as I saw him.

The next morning, I joined Mrs. Ruby for breakfast. She asked me how I felt? I said that I just had stomach pains still, but that I would be fine. We had breakfast. Mr. Jones and Mr. Ron had headed off to the fields already, but Mrs. Ruby said that my brother was still here and wanted to speak with me.

I joined him. He said that we could talk outside, by the pond. When we sat, I told him about Ben, that he was a slave on that plantation. I described how, that when I called out to him he pretended as if I had mistaken him, but that it was him without doubt.

"Please say nothing more to Ben. Talking to him would only endanger you both." "And be sure to stay near the house. We'll be leaving tomorrow morning," he said.

I knew that he was right about Ben, but, no less, I missed him with my whole heart. I spent most rest of the evening dining and talking with Mrs. Ruby. She had started to feel like family.

After supper, I lay in my bed and could think only of Ben, of how broken he seemed, a man different than he, with whom I had fallen in love. In my mind's eye, I could still see the scars on his arm, from the beating that Young Massa Roberts had given him … and how he could not even look at me. I cried and prayed for him—knowing that I would most likely, never see him again.

Morning came, and I joined Mrs. Ruby for our last breakfast together. We said farewells and I told her that I would remember her always.

Mr. Ron sent slaves to fetch our horses as we headed to the wagon. And there again, leading the horses, was Ben. Our eyes met but moments. It was him truly—his eyes told me. He then turned his eyes away. We never spoke, and no one had even noticed our glances. I had never seen eyes so empty, and would never ever forget them.

James and I mounted the wagon and left. Although Ben would always have a place in my heart—I never looked back.

CHAPTER 20

After several months of travel, we arrived at the north. There northern towns were big and busy, and full of movement, with people. James and I had stopped between many inns along the way. To my content, I saw few negroes in the north, and, when I did, I was amazed to see them living freely and making their own way!

My brother said, that we had nearly arrived at the ship that would take us from here. "Maybe another two weeks, at most, until we reach the shore. And, from there, it'll be another month or so of sea travel. After that, we will have made it, Belle," he said.

My brother looked wearier each day. The travelling seemed to have taken its toll on him. Though, he said that once we boarded the ship, we would have nothing but time to rest. That sounded nice—a good, long rest was just the medicine we needed.

I had no idea how it would be to ride on a boat, and so, I began to have a strange mix of feelings. However, I was overjoyed to know that our travels would soon be at an end, that we would soon settle into our new lives. I quietly thanked the Lord.

We arrived at long last to the sea town, where our ship awaited. James said that once we arrived in England, that there was a town called Liverpool. There, we would open our baked goods shop and make a fine life for ourselves. He said that we would need only to purchase supplies when we arrived, that he had already bought a small shop in Liverpool, with rooms in the back where we would live. I would sell breads, and sweet rolls, and maybe even dresses. My brother was a very wise business man, for he seemed to have thought of everything.

The boat would not leave for four days. James decided that we would rest at an inn until then. During our stay at the inn, James felt unwell and took to his bed. He asked if I would run to the shops and restock our supplies. I said yes.

I walked the town without bother. The town seemed to sit right on the ocean's edge. The water was dotted with boats of all kinds, and the pier busy with fisherman and traders. The smell of the ocean sat heavy atop the town. I bought the food and supplies without any problems, and returned to the inn to find James asleep. Over the next few days, James's health only worsened, until he was hardly able to leave his bed, but, no less, he managed to make sure that everything was set and settled before we had left.

James told me of the things we would do and see once aboard the ship. He said, "You'll be quartered in a small cabin with another young woman, who would also be traveling to Liverpool—same with me." When we arrived, we would find our shop by its numbers on the building, he also said, that, in a case where something happened to him—God forbid—the ownership of the shop was not only in his name, but mine, too. The shop had been paid for in total. All that would be left was the purchase of supplies needed to run the shop. At last, we would have a place, to call our own.

When morning came, my brother's illness had not improved. I asked how he felt. Tired, he only returned, but he managed himself up, for the day had come when the ship would quit the shore, and set off. As we made our way across the docks, we came upon it—a boat massive size, that it seemed to burden the water. As we got closer, I could feel my stomach folding.

Men, at the foot of the ship, were checking people's papers before allowing passage.

Even knowing, that our papers and tickets were all accounted for properly, it took all I could to keep calm. What if they had been keeping a close eye out for runaway slaves, I thought to myself.

"Belle," said my brother, taking note of my panic "breathe." He reached down into his sack and removed a container. "Here, have a drink of this. It'll help you to put your feelings at ease. Remember Belle, just act normal."

We boarded the ship without problems. And so, we had come to the last part of our journey.... James and I found our cabins. They seemed, more like a cloak room than a cabin. With two sleeping cots, and a water pitcher, and basin for washing in. There was scarcely space to move about, nor for my baggage. The lady with whom I would be sharing my cabin had not yet arrived, and in such a tight space for a month, I thought it necessary, that we took well to one another.

When she arrived, I learned that her name was Rebecca and that she was twenty-nine. She said she was traveling to Liverpool because it was, in fact, her hometown. She was returning home to see her parents, and to help with her mother, who had taken ill. She said that she had come to America to be married, but that her husband eventually died of illness, and, that when she arrived, she would help her father tend to her sickly mother, allowing her father's attention to return to his trade business.

It seemed we would get along perfectly fine.

We had been travelled near a week. In that time, my brother's health improved little. His thirty-second birthday came while aboard the ship—though rest was his only celebration. He had no appetite and started to appear thinner. The ship had no doctor, only a passenger, who happened to be an off-duty nurse. I begged her to look at him. She agreed. She said that he just needed rest and nourishment, though nothing too solid—like soup. I tended to James as needed, and, when I did not, he spent his time resting.

Rebecca and I had become good friends and had come to depend on one another for support, in fact. One morning, Rebecca said, "I spoke with the Captain today. He said the ship will be stopping soon to resupply. When we are docked, we can find a doctor to see to your brother."

This was good news. James was getting no better, and I had begun to worry unto sickness myself.

There were people of all sort aboard the ship—men, women, and children. Some quartered in small cabins, like Rebecca's and mine, but most passed their nights and days in the common area. I met a woman, Martha, travelling with her two young sons, who intended to rejoin her husband who was a fisherman in Liverpool. Martha and her sons stayed in the common area. Rebecca and I tried to offer her some kindness by allowing her to wash up in our cabin as she pleased—for a woman, this was a long trip to go without a private place to wash or change clothes.

Our second week, the ship docked into an island port to resupply. Rebecca went inland to find a doctor, who would come and look at my brother. She did. The Doctor said James was sick with fever. He said, that we should keep close watch over him for now, and he gave me medicine to help him, but warned that James's sickness had spread badly, and that he was unsure if the medicine could help at this point. I said we would try it besides.

The medicine the Doctor gave James offered little to his recovery. I began to fear the worst. Each night, I cried myself to sleep at the thought of losing my brother. How I could ever go on without him, I did not know. Rebecca offered what support she could, explained that her dad's trade business was well off; that when we arrived, I would have whatever money I needed to aid my brother's recovery. I thanked her for the good friend she been.

I looked after James each day, doing best to clean him and keep him warm, feeding him whenever he was able, to hold down. James had turned over to me all the papers, bank notes, and money, seemed he expected the worse also. This could only be some tease of the devil, I thought and prayed always for God's mercy.

The third week, my brother slipped into a coma. I ran to the nurse and asked her to see to him. He was dying, she said, and there was no more we could do to stop it. She said that he likely would not make it to the end of the trip. Rebecca tried to offer comfort, but I wept each night. The Captain had my brother moved to the sick bay. There, I saw Martha and learned that her youngest boy was sick, too.

Two days after they moved him, my brother died.

As we gathered to mourn and say our last goodbyes, they had my brother's body wrapped. Then, they dropped him overboard—right with my heart.

For days after my brother's death, I did not leave my cabin. I could think of no ways, to continue without my brother. Rebecca, who had kept sure that I ate and cleaned, one morning asked if I would be willing to give the remaining medicine—that the Doctor had given James—to Martha's youngest son. He was sick still, and she believed the medicine might help. I said yes, and just days later, Rebecca shared news that the medicine was helping, that Martha's son had nearly healed. And for the first time since my brother's death, I had hope and a glint of happiness.

As time aided my recovery, I started to sort and put order to the papers my brother had given me, to be set for my arrival. I was to start a new life and business, as I remembered. The Lord had kept me all this way; I could not stop now—for James. And although my heart was burdened with grief, I felt James may have watched over still and would not have wanted, for me to quit now. We had traveled too long, and too far.

The ship had nearly reached the shores of Liverpool. There was much that remained unknown to me, but I knew one thing certainly: that I would make the best of this opportunity James had given me. In that moment, the perfect name for my bakery fell on me: "Roberts Baked Goods" … in memory of where I had come from and the family that I had lost.

I may be alone, but I had found a great friend in Rebecca. She offered me a place to stay until I had finished preparations for my bake shop. Aboard the ship, I had also become friends with Martha, who offered to help me in what ways she could, too. My family may have been lost, but, in their stead, the Lord had blessed me with new, kindhearted friends. And for this, I thanked him.

CHAPTER 21

When only days away from arriving, a great storm struck the ship, tossing the boat as a rag doll. We were all told to remained in the bottom of the ship until the storm had passed. I began to pray for everyone on board. To calm myself, I began writing in my journal—which, in my mind, helped me place things firmly in the past and move on from them. (I wished often that I had children with whom I could leave my writings, so that they would have a chance to learn their history—but I did not. I could only hope that, some way my journal fell into the good hands of someone, who would cherish my story.)

At last, we arrived and docked in Liverpool. Rebecca's family was waiting there to return her home. Before that, she told me that she would help me find my shop. As we rode, I noticed that boats, small and big, lined the docks, and noticed the fisherman and trading that was going on. Farther in town, I noticed the many buildings, shops, and houses which seemed almost stacked atop one another. People strolled all about, tending to their business, quite a busy town—yet seemingly friendly, given that, most people offered happy greetings to one another as they passed on the streets. I had not seen any negro slaves and wondered if maybe they were working inside the homes.

We found the shop. It looked as if it had been owned before. We went inside and found the place in good shape. There were counters and glass cases in which food could be shown. We walked to the back rooms, which I would likely use to sleep and sit in. There were four rooms altogether. I imagined how lovely the place would be—after a bit of cleaning and maybe some draperies to the windows. Rebecca agreed that it was nice, and said she would help however she could.

Later, I accepted Rebecca's offer to stay with her family, just until I had prepared the back rooms of my shop well enough for me to live in. It would but a few weeks, I thought. James had left me with the ownership papers and the money necessary to get started. He had planned things perfectly. It broke my heart that he was not there to see it all, but I would no less make him proud.

We arrived at Rebecca's family home, just outside of town. It is a big house, with a wide front porch and sitting benches to both sides of the front door, and lovely flower beds, to the front and side of the house. As we rode up, a negro man servant came out to take care of the horses and wagon on which we rode in.

Rebecca's father, Mr. Irwin, met and welcomed us as we entered the house, and told me that I was welcome to stay, for long as I needed. Mr. Irwin was an old, friendly—bald—man, with a soft smile and a jolly laugh. His wife, Mrs. Alice, sat in their pallor with a blanket upon her lap. She welcomed us, too. There were also three negro servant women at work about the house. To all shock and disbelief, Rebecca said that they were paid servants, not slaves. As I had learned over time, outwardly, I showed no emotion to this news. Liverpool was far different than where I had escaped from. I guessed that this was why James had picked this, of all places, to live.

I had been staying with Rebecca and her family for a bit past a week, each day travelling into town to clean and prepare my shop for opening. Rebecca's father had given me a bed and other things to furnish the back rooms. I offered to pay him for them, but he refused, he said that they were gifts. I thanked him—and the Lord. Now, I had all that I needed to live in my shop.

One morning, while shopping for baking supplies, I came across Martha and her youngest son. We hugged and spoke with one another. We talked of how my shop was coming along and the kinds of bake goods I would sell, that I intended to sell homemade breads, rolls, cakes, and even cookies. I told her that I considered also of making dresses and aprons, as ordered. Martha asked if I needed help in the shop with the baking? I said yes, and she offered to work with me, saying that she baked well, too.

She said she could teach me to make tea cakes, which were popular in England. I welcomed her help with open arms. I thanked God that I now had someone to work alongside me. In that moment, it seemed that all the troubles of my past, could not cast a shadow on my joy. When I got back to Rebecca's family home I told her of the good news, that Martha would be working with me. Her family was happy for me. I missed my brother so much and I was truly sad that he was not here, to see all his hard work take place. I learned to accept that the Lord knows what's best. My bake shop was nearly ready to open for business. I needed a few more supplies that I had ordered from the main store. So, I had to travel to town when they came in.

As I was picking up the last of my supplies, I came across a child begging in the streets for food. He looked to be nine or ten ... his clothes torn and tattered. I approached and asked him where had his mother gone to.

"My mother is dead and my father was a fisherman, who went away and never came back. Can you spare me some bread please?" he said.

My eyes watered at this. I told him that I would give him food, as soon as I came out of the store. I asked what was his name and his age?

"Edmund," he said, "and I'm ten."

"Edmund, would you wait until I get back from the store?" I asked.

He agreed.

While I was in the store, I continued to think of that boy, with no mother or father, and having to beg strangers for food. He hadn't a place to live, either. I decided that I would offer him room and board in my shop, if he wanted to. And in return, he could help with keeping the place clean. When I came out, I gave the boy food to eat. I told him of my offer, which he accepted gladly. The Lord had helped me so much in life, that it was only fair I that I gave that same help, and kindness to someone in need of it.

My baked shop opened and did well the first day. Rebecca's family had put word out all over town of my opening. The smells of the breads and cakes, brought people from all around which contribute to my success of the first day. I could sense my brother smiling down from Heaven.

No one had ever questioned me being, as a free white woman. I would hold tight the secret of my true self until my death—not because I was ashamed of who I was, but because I was ashamed of how negro people were treated, and I no longer could suffer it. And because I could not help the body I was born to. I would have to spend the rest of my life hiding in plain sight.

CHAPTER 22

The Bake shop had done well the past couple years. Edmund, the boy I took in, became like a son to me. He worked hard always. I had fixed the four back rooms, two became bedrooms, one for sitting, and sewing dresses and aprons, and the last a room for washing in. It had become a comfortable home, for Edmund and I. I knew that if his father ever returned, he would likely go with him. Though, in my heart, I felt that no one would ever come for him—and no one ever did.

Martha was still with me. She and I worked well together. She had showed me how to make tea cakes, and, in return, I showed her how to make rolls and meal breads that sold well, also. Word of mouth helped bring people from all walks to my shop. My years went by peacefully.

Rebecca met a man, they fell in love, they married. She decided to return with him to his hometown, still in England, but not Liverpool. She and I had become very close, like sisters, and I cried when she left. She promised to visit me often as she could.

I have not written in my journal for thirteen years now, and I am forty-seven in age. I have become very sick with an illness called smallpox, and I am near death. I have been moved to a rest place, surrounded by the sick and dying—my own kind. I know that I am soon to leave this world.

I have raised Young Edmund to be a good, honest man. He is twenty-five and has taken a wife, Hannah. They have been married for five years. They both take good care of the bake shop, along with Martha. Martha's sons have become fishermen, like their father, and all have families of their own. My dear Rebecca, she has two boys. She still comes to visit now and then.

I have gotten to live out the rest of my days as a free woman—a true blessing. I have seen cities, and towns, and countries, also the ocean. Which is more than my mother or grandmother ever had the chance to see.

There are times when I wonder if Young Massa Roberts still lives, and if he ever learned of his brother's death. I even prayed for him sometimes. I have suffered a time now with this sickness, but I dare not complain. My life, here in Liverpool, has been better than I ever imagined it would be.

I was born a negro slave, but blessed with freedom. And so, I will leave this world in unbroken peace and thankfulness—hoping soon to be reunited with those I have lost.

THE END.

ABOUT THE AUTHOR

Mrs. C. Evans was born in California. As a young child, her parents moved to Chicago, Illinois, where she was raised. She now resides in Northwest Indiana. Mrs. C. Evans worked in the home-health field for twenty years until she became disabled. She is a widowed mother of two sons and grandmother of five. When she is not writing, she volunteers for her community through the Froebel Community Council, an organization that provides a monthly prayer breakfast, a yearly back-to-school fest, and a neighborhood cleanup drive. She attends the Gethsemane Missionary Baptist Church, where she is a member of their choir and chairman of their programs committee. This is Mrs. C. Evans's first published work. Because of the inspiration this story has given her, she continues her passion and goals for writing. She is currently working on her second manuscript for publication.

Printed in the United States
By Bookmasters